CASE of the WACKY CAT

Written by Elizabeth Bolton

Illustrated by Paul Harvey

Troll Associates

Library of Congress Cataloging in Publication Data

Bolton, Elizabeth.
  Case of the wacky cat.

  Summary: Kim and David, neighborhood detectives,
help Mrs. Rumpleberry find her missing cat.
    1. Children's stories, American. [1. Mystery and
detective stories] I. Harvey, Paul, 1926-   ill.
II. Title.
PZ7.B63597Cas   1985   [E]   84-8725
ISBN 0-8167-0400-7 (lib. bdg.)
ISBN 0-8167-0401-5 (pbk.)

BABY

Mrs. Rumpleberry was so upset. She just stood with the brass dinner bell in her hand and wailed.

"Oh, my poor Baby!" she cried. "He must be in terrible trouble. Otherwise he'd *never* miss his supper."

Baby was Mrs. Rumpleberry's cat. He
was big and round and striped like a tiger.
He liked to go exploring for hours. But he
always came home for supper.

Kim and Dave looked at each other. This was their big chance! They had always wanted to be detectives. Dave had red hair and glasses and was very nosy. Kim lived next door. She had two brown braids and was very smart.

Dave puffed out his chest. "We now have a Lost Cat Case," he said. He pushed his glasses up higher on his nose and started looking around.

Kim handed Mrs. Rumpleberry some lemonade. "Think about when you saw Baby last," she said. But Mrs. Rumpleberry was not much help.

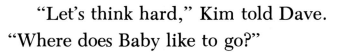

"Let's think hard," Kim told Dave. "Where does Baby like to go?"

"He likes to go up in the maple tree," Dave said.

"He also likes to go stare at the other cats on the corner," said Kim.

"He likes to go to Mr. Rancini's butcher shop."

"He likes to climb in car windows and take naps in the back seat."

"He likes to eat *ice cream*," they both agreed.

First, Dave climbed the maple tree. But Baby wasn't there. Then Kim and Dave looked through the open windows of Dave's mother's car. Baby wasn't inside.

At Kim's house the garage door was open.
"*Hmmm,*" thought Dave. He looked inside
the extra tires and behind the lawn mower.
But he didn't find Baby. Dave stood on tiptoe

to look behind the oil cans on the shelf.
He looked in the grass seed, and in some
paint cans.

All at once he heard a voice behind him. "David," said Kim's mother, "can't you find enough trouble to get into at your own house?"

Dave pushed his glasses up higher on his nose. "We're detecting," he explained. "We're on the Case of the Rumpleberry Cat."

"Well you won't find him in our paint
cans," said Kim's mother with a smile.

Kim grabbed Dave's hand and pulled him
away. "Come on. Let's look down the street."

At the corner, a gray cat and a
tan cat were holding a staring match.
But Baby wasn't there.

Kim and Dave turned down Maple Street.
Mr. Rancini was cranking the awning at the
butcher shop. He wiped his hands on his
white apron.

"Mr. Rancini, have you seen Baby?" asked Kim. "We're trying to find him."

"Baby hasn't been here today," said Mr. Rancini. "I saved him some scraps, too. But I haven't seen him. Why not look out back? Sometimes he knocks the lid off my trash can and climbs inside."

The lid was off Mr. Rancini's can. But Baby wasn't in it.

Kim and Dave looked at each other. "Let's try the ice-cream store," Dave said. Kim nodded.

The bell on the door tinkled as they went inside. The air smelled like cherries and lemon and root beer. Kim loved to come here. She liked to sit on one of the high stools and talk to Mr. Jones behind the counter.

Dave loved to look at the unusual toys and
things in the showcase. Mr. Jones always had
something new to show them. Today there
was a magnifying glass.

"Just what I need," said Dave, staring at
Kim through the magnifying glass. Kim
stared back and made a funny face.

22

Kim took the lemonade money from her pocket. Mr. Jones made them each an ice-cream cone. But he couldn't tell them where Baby was.

"Baby likes to lick the empty ice-cream barrels. I give them to him in the alley. But I haven't seen him at all today. Try next door. He likes to visit there."

ICE CREAM

The dress shop next door had white
ribbons around the window. Sunlight fell
through the window onto a beautiful dress.
It glittered and twinkled with little silver
beads. Kim wished she could try it on.

dresses

25

Then she remembered she had to be a
detective first.

"Come on, Detective Kim," Dave said
gruffly. He was trying to sound like a
detective on TV.

A woman came to meet them. She looked
worried about their ice-cream cones. But
when she heard why they were there, she
smiled. "Baby comes here often. He likes to
sleep in my window. The sun makes him
cozy warm. But I haven't had to chase him
out today."

They thanked her and went outside.
"We have to think some more," Kim said.
"What does Baby *really* like to do?"

Dave thought hard. "Baby likes to pretend he's a tiger," he said at last. "He likes to chase squirrels. He likes to chase butterflies. He likes to fight."

"He likes to get into things," Kim said slowly. She looked at Dave. "Come on!" she shouted, and started to run.

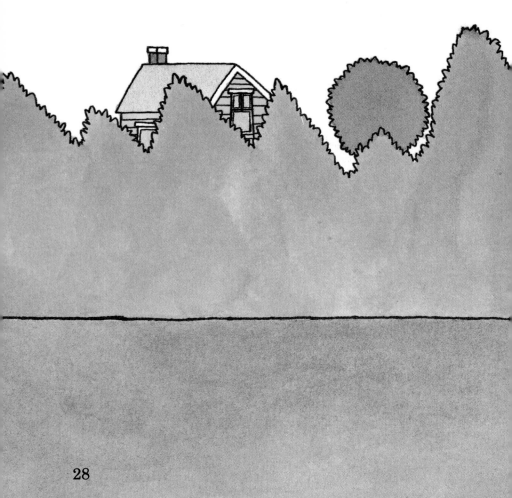

Dave ran to catch up. "Where are we going?" he panted.

"Back to Mrs. Rumpleberry's house," said Kim. "That's where she missed him."

Mrs. Rumpleberry's gate was still open.
Baby wasn't swinging on it. Baby wasn't on
the porch railing. Mrs. Rumpleberry was still
ringing the dinner bell and wailing.

"First, we'll look in the bushes," Kim
said. But Baby wasn't there. Next, Dave
crawled under the porch. He pretended he

was an explorer in a cave. He found a peach
pit and a garter snake and a friendly turtle.
But Baby wasn't there either.

"It's getting dark," moaned Mrs. Rumpleberry. "You two have to go home and eat. Poor Baby isn't getting any supper. Oh dear, oh dear! Oh my...my...my."

"Please, Mrs. Rumpleberry," Kim said. "*Think*. What did you do when you were in the house today?"

Mrs. Rumpleberry ran her fingers through her hair.

"I watered the geraniums," she said. "I did the laundry. I tried on my new hat. I had a chocolate cookie. I put the strawberries in the refrigerator."

She turned pink. "And I jumped rope. It's very good for your nerves, you know, jumping rope."

"Don't worry, Mrs. Rumpleberry," Kim said kindly. "We'll find Baby for you."

A window at Kim's house went up. Kim's
mother leaned out. "In *five minutes*,"
she called, "come home for dinner."

Kim pretended she hadn't heard. She led
Dave and Mrs. Rumpleberry upstairs into the
Rumpleberry house. They looked on the
closet shelf and in the box with Mrs.
Rumpleberry's new hat. They looked under

the bed. They looked in the bathtub. They
looked into and under and on top of all sorts
of things. They found Baby's rubber mouse
and three pencils and seven hairpins, but no
Baby.

They went downstairs. Dave looked in the refrigerator. "He wouldn't be there," Kim said. "It's too cold. Baby likes to be warm."

"That's right," said Mrs. Rumpleberry. "He got his tail shut once in the refrigerator door. He wouldn't want it to happen again."

"There are some nice pickles in here, though," said Dave hungrily.

Mrs. Rumpleberry gave him one. "Anything you would like, my dear?" she asked Kim.

"I'd like—to see—the laundry room,"
Kim said slowly.

"That's silly," Dave said. "Baby doesn't
like to be wet. He likes to be warm."

"*Kimberly Marie!*" Kim's mother called
from next door. "COME HOME!"

"Baby likes to be warm," said Kim in that careful voice. "The woman at the dress shop said so. He likes to sleep where it's nice and cozy warm."

She sprang to the laundry basket, still full of warm, fluffy clothes.

There snuggled in the fresh towels was a fat, tiger-striped ball of fur.

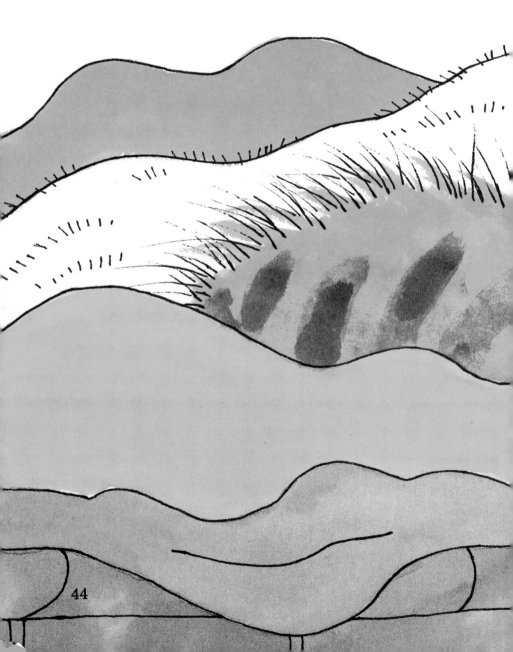

"My goodness!" Mrs. Rumpleberry cried. "He must have jumped in there when I took the dry clothes out. How silly of me!"

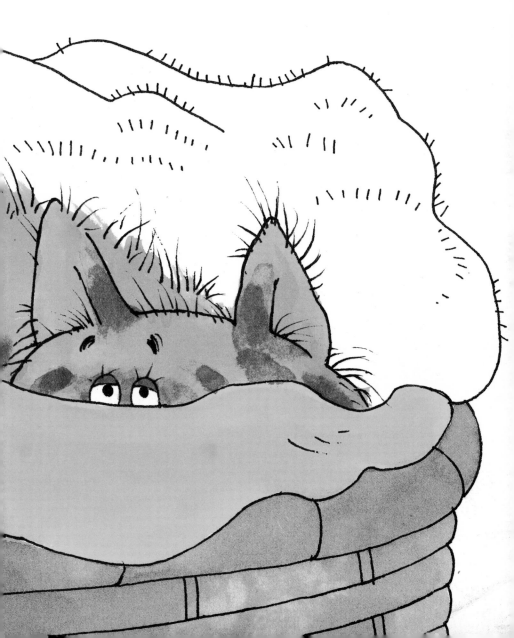

She scooped Baby up and hugged him.
Baby had been dreaming about chasing mice.
He didn't like being woken up. But he didn't
mind at all when he saw his dinner.

"My goodness, what would I do without you two detectives?" asked Mrs. Rumpleberry. She passed the cookie jar.

Kim and Dave shook hands with her.
"Call on us any time," Dave said, munching
a cookie. "We're always ready to solve a
mystery—especially when the reward tastes
this good!"

They went home to dinner. But they
didn't tell their mothers about the cookies.